Imposs-i-Bella

ImpossiBella
A Flip-Flopped Fairy Tale

By Savannah Verte

Published by
Eclectic Bard Books
USA

Cover design: AM Creations, 2017.

ISBN: 978-1974618385 (Trade Paperback)
AISN: B074FH4FWV (Amazon)

DEDICATION

This book is affectionately dedicated to the members of the
'If Wylie Coyote can do it, I can too' club.
Also, to those who find joy in the quirks…because in so
many places & times…they are where the living happens.
To you.

Marialee—
Thanks for stopping!
Enjoy the read!!
Savannah.

Acknowledgements

This page always buckles me under. I'd honestly need another book to list everyone who should be acknowledged for things. The drive to continue writing is always influenced by others.

SO, this time, I'll make it simple.

One, to AM Creations who had this absolutely insane cute cover that drove me. I HAD to write a tale for it.

AND,

Two, to Hay Hay Scully who named my Fairy Godmothers here. Not knowing the story, she suggested the monikers, and I for one think she hit them SPOT ON!

Chapter 1

Flora took in the scene from her alcove near the window, staying to the periphery. The baby to be born would be her charge. Judging by the state of the grand affair, this child would not need her. People were tripping over themselves to offer goods and services to the family, though the family wasn't in the room. By her count, it was about time she got an easy case anyway. Being a Fairy Godmother was hard work.

The child wailed a blistering scream just after the resounding smack across its bottom was heard. Wincing, she had to give it credit, the child had lungs. Flora withdrew her fingers from her ears after several moments and waited for the pronouncement.

"It's a girl." Was announced loudly to the waiting crowd in the ante-chamber beyond the birthing quarter's door, by a less than enthusiastic servant whose head disappeared just as abruptly as it had appeared. The crowd erupted.

It was not a secret. The house desperately needed a female young if there was to be any hope of salvaging the family name. Generations of males had all but run the reputation into the ground. A stockpile had been secreted away ages ago for just this moment. Before long, there would be pledges and promises, and a handsome dowry to a male of worth. Flora wondered off-hand whom would be chosen, and just how long it might take. She guessed the marriage bargain would be made before the child could walk.

Hours later, the young's moniker was announced as the child was presented; Isabella Reede Esme Catherine Renee Beaufort. Flora decided immediately that she would call her Bella. That was that.

Approaching the parents once they appeared, Flora bowed and gave her blessings, introduced herself, and left for the nursery to await the child. There was no need to linger, she knew exactly what was coming. A great vat of wine had already been opened and was being poured long before the family emerged from the birthing chambers. There would be drinking and merriment, singing and speculating, posturing and promises…then there would be a screaming child delivered to the nursery. Flora was going to get her break before she couldn't.

As expected, the girl arrived shortly, wailing for all she was worth in the arms of the nursemaid. Flora inspected her carefully, knowing immediately that her earlier assessment was wrong, this child would be a handful, her obsidian eyes twinkled with mischief already. It did not escape Flora's notice that this child was her own nemesis as she had cleaved a tuft of her own hair and was pulling.

"No wonder you're wailing. I'd cry too if someone were tugging at my hair." She chided the squalling baby.

"I hardly think…" the nursemaid began, cutting herself short when she noticed whom she addressed. "I beg your pardon. Would you care to hold her?"

"No, no. I'll leave that to you." Flora retorted with a smug grin as she pointed to her own chest. "Perk of position.

You swaddle and soothe, I get to try to keep her out of trouble for the next eighteen years. I daresay, judging by right now, I'll have my hands plenty full of her before too long. Isn't that right Miss Bella?" She finished her comments to the child directly who almost seemed to narrow her eyes in reply.

The nursemaid didn't seem affronted until Flora called the girl 'Bella,' at which she tried to spin away. "You should at least learn her name." she admonished.

"I know her name." Flora responded softly, even as her hand shot out to halt the spin with force. "But I, unlike you, am not her servant."

The nursemaid's sharp intake of breath was not quiet. "If….if…if you won't help me with her, then perhaps you will give her some peace. Being born into this world has surely exhausted her. You can leave." She said on a raspy, harsh whisper.

Flora laughed loudly. For a moment, Bella quieted at the sound. It was short-lived. Though the child resumed her screaming, Flora's face was calm, nearly stoic, before she spoke. "Hear me clearly; I will leave when I wish, and stay when I wish. And, though you may not always see me, I am watching. I do not answer to you any more than I answer to the child in your arms. Do you understand?"

The maid nodded mutely, her jaw slack at the rebuke.

"I'm glad we cleared that up. And thank you, I do believe I'll go now. This evening has been taxing." Flora announced before turning to leave.

Turning back, she smirked at the maid with an odd giggle. "Silly me…as if I need to leave through the door." She announced before spiraling her finger into the air and disappearing, waiting until she was out of sight to laugh at the expression on the maid's face as she went. She only narrowly managed it. The sound bubbled up to her lips with such force she nearly didn't hold the outburst.

Fern was seated in her favorite chair, flipping the pages of a book she wasn't reading when Flora returned. Her sister was nearly cackling at something, though it was in conflict with the steam that seemed to rise off of her in thick tufts.

"Whatever is going on?" Fern queried as she looked up.

"Just enjoying the reaction." Flora retorted off-hand, waving off further questions.

Fern studied her, not taking the hint. "You got your new assignment then did you?"

"You know I did." Flora quipped, almost snapping the words out. "You're next you know." She wagged a finger.

"Yes, I know." Fern said calmly, turning yet another page she wasn't looking at. "I believe it will be tomorrow though. Maybe."

"What makes you say that?" Flora glared.

Fern heaved a hard sigh and closed the book. "It's not going well. Breech."

Flora gasped at the one word that said it all. "We can share mine." She offered lamely.

Fern shrugged it off. "We'll see."

Chapter 2

Ariella Engeneu arrived in the early hours of the morning following Harvest Eve, after a long and difficult labor that claimed her mother's life. It was quiet in the room. The guests for the birthing had dispersed hours before when it seemed that the child would be born still. Fern had remained, veiled in the corner, waiting to see what would be. She heaved a heavy breath of relief to hear the child's soft cries.

To his credit, the father took the child from the maid and asked to be left alone. Fern nearly broke at the heart-wrenching scene. The babe was laid alongside her mother's now lifeless, though still warm, body. The proud, stoic male broke then, weeping openly, making promises to his wife and child.

Fern waited until the scene was ended and the maid called to return. She slipped from the birthing room to wait in the parlor while arrangements were made for the young woman who had not survived. She decided this child would need her.

Stepping gently to his side, once the father had returned, Fern introduced herself and offered her blessings. The response was kind, even as the eyes spoke louder. "I am relieved. I do not know what I will do now. I've never raised a girl." He admitted.

"Pish-posh. You'll manage. I'm sure of it." Fern clipped brightly.

"Do you think any would have me now?" He enquired, slumped over with his head in his hands.

"Any who would have you?" Fern asked, leaning in to

hear his muffled words.

"I will have to remarry."

"There's time. I'm here, as are others. I'm sure you can wait awhile for that."

"'Riella will need a woman's interventions." He bemoaned loudly.

"What am I? Chopped liver?" Fern retorted, trying to lighten the overwhelming load.

He looked up. "No. You are a Fairy Godmother. It's different."

"We'll see about that." Fern nodded to give weight to her words, even as she knew he was right. She would be walking a very slim line to be anything more to this child.

Just about that time, the maid re-emerged with the now clean and swaddled babe. He held out his arms to cradle his child. Fern wished she had the magic to make this right, but knew she did not as she looked over his shoulder at the girl.

She was tiny, so tiny, Fern thought to herself. This little girl was delicate, just as her mother had been. The little girl's green eyes danced and twinkled in response to her father's soft cooing. He would be a good parent. Fern knew that much. He would have to be, for both of them.

When the blanket slipped, Fern let out a soft gasp to see a shock of strawberry blonde hair tufting from her head, lighter, but definitely that of her father. *Good.* She thought to herself, perhaps seeing a bit of himself in his child will help.

His soft chuckles broke through a moment later. "I…I hadn't noticed that before." He stammered.

"I'm sure there will be many things you come to notice, that you didn't see before." Fern consoled, knowing that his thoughts had been directed elsewhere initially. "It's only been a few hours."

"And yet it feels like a lifetime already." He replied, pulling his bundle closer as he finished.

"Because in some ways, it has been." Fern offered. "But, this lifetime," she nodded toward the girl, "her lifetime…is just begun."

His eyes were full of emotion when he looked up to her standing above him. "So it has."

He looked back and forth between Fern and the child several times before continuing. "Thank you for staying when everyone else departed. I'm grateful to have gotten to share her arrival with someone."

"My duty, my privilege, and my great joy to be here to see this beauty arrive and be welcomed. I'll always be near to aid her as I'm able." Fern genuflected.

"We are both blessed to have you."

Fern flopped into her favorite chair as she arrived. Flora frowned immediately. "Need to share mine?" She enquired.

"No. The baby arrived safely." Flora announced, sounding as excited as a dead fish.

"Then, why the long face?"

"The baby made it. The mother didn't." Fern lamented, her shoulders slumped. "I'm afraid the future is going to be difficult for this little one, and I find I am upset that I cannot do more for her. Rules only bend so far you know."

Flora's head tipped from side to side studying her sister. "Oh no you don't. I know that look, and your words give it emphasis. You ***cannot*** do anything more. You know this."

"Of course I know this. Why do you think I'm so miserable? This sweet, innocent, little girl has just arrived and already she has to learn loss. Am I to act like that doesn't matter?" Fern sniffled back emotions that were too close to breaking the surface.

"Yes. Yes you are." Flora rebuked harshly, wagging her finger in Fern's face. "You must remember your place, and it is as her Fairy Godmother, nothing more."

Fern sighed, wiped a stray tear, and squared her shoulders. "I will. I always do. Just once though, I'd like to have an easy one."

Flora laughed loudly. "I was thinking the very same thing about my cases. Perhaps we should switch."

Fern gasped. "You know that's not allowed."

"I know. It doesn't mean I don't wish for it."

Chapter 3

True to prediction, before Bella's first birthday came near, a marriage proposition had been made, and confirmed. Bella was promised to Prince Christopher Leopold, though the two had never met, and wouldn't for many years. The family was ecstatic at their good fortune.

The arrangement was fairly standard for the time. When Bella turned sixteen, she would meet her betrothed. Until then, she would be raised, and groomed, for her eventual assent to the throne. The marriage planning began the day the proposed arrangement was affirmed. Flora thought she might be ill most days hearing about the outlandish preparations to be completed. The words 'over the top' came to mind often.

Years blended one into the next as Bella grew, and grew to be more snobbish and difficult than could have been foreseen.

"Flora, come play with me. Flora, I want a pony. Flora, make me pretty. Flora, I'll be queen one day, you should bow." Came from the petulant child's whining mouth on repeat. Flora was having none of it.

"Bella, go play outside. Bella, ask your father. Bella, that's not my place. Bella, I am not your servant." She retorted to each new demand, trying desperately to keep her tone neutral and calm.

"I can't go outside to play. There's no one to play with me. It's impossible."

"It's not."

"I'll never be pretty unless you do something. It's

impossible. Do your magic and make it happen. I know you can."

"Can is not the issue."

"You're impossible."

"Yes. Perhaps, that's it." Flora retorted bating. "I'm the impossible one."

When she was ten, Bella tripped up the stairs before falling back down, breaking her leg in two places. Flora was not nearby when it happened, but that didn't prevent her from being blamed.

"Flora didn't stop it." Bella wailed to her parents.

"Florrrrahhhhh!" the summons boomed.

Stunned, Flora appeared, confused at what had happened when she arrived. For a moment anyway, until the charges were leveled.

"You are her Fairy Godmother. Are you not?" Bella's father demanded.

"Yes."

"And you swore to keep her safe when she was born, did you not?" Bella's mother added before Flora finished answering.

"No." Flora replied adamantly.

"Yes. You. Did." Bella screamed.

"No. I did not." Flora responded, reaching deep for a soft voice. "I gave you my blessing and endeavored to keep you out of trouble. I did not, vow to keep you safe from harming yourself. I did not, agree to make you pretty. I did not, promise to give you whatever you want, whenever you want. I did not, consent to be your playmate, or your servant. I did not."

Three stunned faces reddened with each new thing itemized that Flora was not there to do. Bella recovered first.

"Then what good are you? What do we need you for? I am injured. You did nothing to prevent it. Can you fix it? If not, you are dismissed."

Flora resisted the temptation to lash out. She knew well what was within her powers, though this was not about ability now. This was about choice. She would not be goaded into it. Determined, she set her face carefully before she replied.

"If you have no need of me, then I will abide your wishes and take my departure." She said simply before raising a finger to wisp herself away.

Bella was obviously furious. "You can't fix it? What good are you? You never do what I want." She wailed.

Flora dropped her finger for a moment. "Oh, yes of course I can." She paused, wanting to savor the moment as she watched the hope bloom. She was going to enjoy far too much watching it dashed. "But, I'm not going to."

Before another word could be uttered, she raised her finger again, gave it a spin, and disappeared as Bella's mouth opened to scream again. She wasn't upset that she missed whatever words the child chose to spit out next.

Fern returned to find Flora pacing, muttering angrily under her breath. "Rotten, rotten, rotten. Serves her right."

Fern tip-toed in and eased into her seat before Flora noticed her and stopped her diatribe. "Don't look at me like that!" Flora lashed out.

"Look at you like what? I didn't look at you like anything.

I can tell you are upset. I was not about to levy any of that my direction." Fern replied, easing back into the chair with her hands raised before her.

"I apologize." Flora offered, not quite sounding like she meant it.

"Accepted." Fern said without offering or asking for more.

"Are you sure we can't switch?" Flora finally commented.

Fern broke into peals of laughter before she could staunch it. She fought for a few moments to get under control before she was able to respond, knowing that the longer she delayed, the angrier Flora was becoming. "You know we cannot." She finally managed.

Flora uttered an unintelligible shriek.

"Tell me what's happened. Perhaps there is a solution that you cannot see." Fern offered.

"No. There is no solution needed. The brat dismissed me as though she had the right or ability to do so."

"Dismissed?!" Fern gasped out, leaning forward. "No…she didn't."

"She did."

"Why?"

Flora sighed and puddled into a heap on the rug. "Because she was injured, and I wouldn't mend her."

"But…you can mend her." Fern answered, sounding as confused as she actually was.

"Can, yes. Willing to…no." Flora retorted snorting.

"Why?" Fern asked, dragging out the sound.

"Because she needs to learn. She did something that had a consequence, and she wanted me to wave it away like it had never been. She will never understand responsibility if she is not accountable for the results."

"This is true. How injured was she?" Fern asked, trying to understand how significant the issue was.

"Broken bones. Leg bones. One leg. They will heal of their own accord if she actually follows a regimen that allows it. She won't, but she could." Flora cut in. "She wants it fixed immediately, no limitation."

"So she demanded you fix it." Fern offered her understanding.

"Oh no…not just demanded it. She, and her parents, blamed me for it happening to begin with. The assertion was that I had sworn to keep her safe, and I didn't."

Fern gasped in shock, her eyes flying wide. "They didn't…"

"They did."

"Do they know how fortunate they are to have a Fairy Godmother? Not everyone gets one you know."

"Yes Fern, I know that. And, you know that. And, they should know that too…but it is beyond them to believe it." Flora waved off. "It couldn't possibly be anyone else's fault that their spoiled offspring was injured. No matter…they have a magic cure-all, me. Right? That's what we're for, or at least to them."

"Fools." Fern bit out.

"Yes, fools. And so, when I wouldn't, though it was stated as, 'if you can't,' I was dismissed."

Fern shook her head laughing. "That would do it. You dug your heels in and said 'no' then, right?"

"Something like that." Flora grinned.

Fern squirreled her lips in an odd smirk. "Oh, I can just imagine."

"Yeah."

"So, what now?"

"What do you mean, 'what now?' It's not like we get a choice, not really anyway. I have to…I have no idea what I have to do now. But, I know I don't get to trade in for a new assignment."

"Hmmmm." Fern frowned. "No, I suppose that's true."

"Let me just say though, I knew this one was trouble from the off."

"Oh, so that's why you were willing to share?" Fern narrowed her eyes on her sister.

"Maybe."

Chapter 4

Ariella was having growing pains of her own. For the first ten years of her life, it had been just her and her father. She was content to sit near him in the evenings as he hunched over papers at the table, asking intermittently about her days. She didn't know she was missing anything.

He felt the weight though of trying to be both parents and eventually took another wife. He married a woman of status who was widowed with two daughters of her own. They were just older than Ariella. He married for purpose, not for love this time, intent to have a mother figure for his growing child. Ariella felt the shift immediately.

In the beginning the façade was maintained. Her stepmother acted the part of doting mother when her father was around. But when he was gone, there was no illusion of affection, from her, or her daughters. Ariella's good nature and willingness to help around the house was no longer about choice. She was given the lion's share of the work-load, and little help.

Her father, weighted with the added responsibility of three more mouths to feed from his table, worked longer and harder to keep up with the lifestyle his new family demanded. It would be his undoing. He worked until he was frail and often in poor health. It still wasn't enough for the added trio, and his wife goaded him to do more still. Ariella was furious, but remained mute.

"We must keep up appearances." She heard her stepmother demanding. "I did not take on raising your child to give up my standing. You knew that from the beginning. Our accounts are thin, and people are talking." She admonished, not knowing Ariella could hear every word.

Ariella wept with pangs of guilt. This was all for her. She was sure her step-sisters could hear it too. She saw the way they looked at her father and snickered behind his back. Nothing he did was good enough for them. She wanted desperately to have him take her away from them. Still, she remained quiet. She was the child, and he was the parent.

Evenings, she would sit near him like she had done when she was smaller, trying to ease his burden any way she could find. Once her tasks were complete, she would sit near the hearth and work her numbers in the soot while he did his on paper. It was the only solace she knew, and mostly the only time she saw him. He was up and gone early, leaving a peck on her cheek before dashing off to work, leaving her behind for the days abuses.

Her step-sisters took to calling her Cinder-iella while her father was away. Eventually, it mutated into Cinderella, though they were careful not to say it when her father was home. Not that they were worried, they knew he would not reprimand them, and if he left it for their mother to do, it would only be for show. Ariella knew it too.

For the things that had changed, one thing did not. Her father loved her more than anything. He didn't often have the material means to show it, but his actions always did. Ariella spent every moment available with him. Somehow she knew, she would not have forever.

That she got a few more years was somehow miraculous. Somewhere in her heart, she knew he was holding on for her. That guilt weighed on her as well. If he could hang on for her, she could do no less for him in return.

It was Fern's turn to pace erratically, cussing out intermittently under her breath. Flora would have laughed if it weren't so out of character for her sister. She opted for what she hoped came across as concern. "What gives? This isn't like you at all."

"She's going to lose him. I can see it coming. I'd bet she can too. As if that sweet girl hasn't had it hard enough, the Fates are going to take him from her too." Fern spat out.

"The father?"

"Yes. It's plain to see. He's not going to last the next winter I'd wager. That woman he married is driving him to his grave, the same as she did the last one with her two arrogant, clueless daughters. It makes me angry."

"I can see that." Flora acknowledged, watching Fern continue wearing a path in the rug. "It's not like you can do anything though. Feels crappy, doesn't it?"

"Don't go all-knowing on me. This is not what you've got going on." Fern hissed.

"No, it isn't remotely. He at least tries. Mine…they think everything happens to them, not because of them. You can't fix that." Flora rationalized from her perch near the bookcase.

"I suppose. But what's the point? Why are we given them? What is it that we are supposed to do, besides go insane a little? I can't stand it. I want to ring their necks through the starched collars they wear." Fern was nearly shouting.

Flora couldn't hold it back any longer, breaking into fits of laughter.

"What's so funny?!" Fern demanded, pausing mid-stride.

"You are Fern. Ring their necks? Really?! How very unbecoming of a Fairy Godmother." Flora teased.

"Well I'm not ***their*** Fairy Godmother." Fern spat back.

"No. No you aren't. THEN you would be in my shoes." Flora rationalized, dodging the airborne shoe that narrowly missed her head.

"That's not even a little bit funny Flora." Fern added before stomping away.

"I'm not trying to be funny. It's the truth. We have opposite sides of the same situation, just with different people. You have a charge, who is genuinely good but is being thumbed under by some really awful people. I have the opposite. I have a really rotten egg who wants everyone, the good ones and the bad, to treat them like they are worthy, when they aren't. The problem for me is, I don't know who the good one is that should get the blessings we have to offer. You at least have that much."

Fern stopped pacing. "You're right. So what do I do about it?"

"I don't know. I wish I did." Flora admitted. "I keep hoping that something happens that makes it clear what should be and how I can affect it to happen. So far, I've got nothing."

"Hurrrumph. Well, let me know if that changes. This is getting ridiculous. What's the point of being a Fairy Godmother if you can't make something good happen? I'd just about turn in my wings if I thought that was an option."

"Don't say things like that." Flora gasped. "You might not get the choice and have them taken away."

"It would be a better thing to be powerless, than to have power and feel powerless." Fern retorted, flopping into her chair. "This is killing me."

"Make that two of us."

Chapter 5

The time to meet the prince had arrived. Bella was sixteen. Flora watched from just beyond vision as the family donned their finery in anticipation of their reception into the royal household, and family. Her stomach lurched listening to them.

"He's going to love you. He'll be so enamored by your beauty, I'll bet they want to move the wedding up to your eighteenth birthday." Her mother cooed.

"He can ask for that. I'll think about it." Bella retorted snidely. "I mean, it is *MY* wedding day, it should be up to me."

For just a moment, Flora wished that using her powers for ill intent were possible, but it wasn't. She was going to have to let this play out. She did not however, have to help. She could do that.

She remained beyond vision for the duration. It was agonizing. She wanted to intervene at multiple points, and had to shift between realms on several others to keep from giving herself away by fits of laughter. The interaction was a disaster from the beginning.

King Maximillian and Queen Constantina were gracious, as was the Prince. That however was where the appropriate behavior ended. Bella and her family tripped over social graces from the door. The King visibly winced when Bella's father called the Prince, 'Son.'

Flora was disappointed. There was no way to watch the adults, and the children at the same time once the Prince and Bella were allowed to be alone to get to know one another. Her duty was to Bella, so she missed whatever happened between the parents from that point on.

She winced to watch Bella look the Prince up and down disapprovingly, as though she had the right.

"Do you always wear your hair like that?" Bella had opened.

The Prince's shock was obvious. "I do. Do you always wear so much stuff on your face?" He recovered to respond, equally antagonistic.

Bella gasped. "What's wrong with my face?" She decried.

"You have too much stuff on it. You look fake." He answered flippantly.

"That is not how a husband speaks to a wife." Bella jabbed back.

"You aren't my wife."

"We are to be married. That means...wife." Bella snipped, stopping her foot and pointing to her chest.

The Prince scratched at his nearly non-existent sideburns. "I don't know about that."

"You don't know about what?" Bella demanded, crossing her arms.

"About you becoming my wife."

"We are promised. Didn't you get told?" Bella asked astonished.

"Oh, I got told. But see, I also got told that it wasn't a done deal, until it was a done deal." He said matter-of-factly, staring her down as her blood stained up her cheeks.

"NO. That's not how this works. I have been promised

to you since before I was one. Your family accepted the proposal. It's a done deal." She asserted through clenched teeth.

His shrug only pushed her further. Flora was fighting to stay for the rest of the scene. She had to duck out again with his next words.

"It might have been then, but times change. I'm my own person. I didn't accept your proposal, and seeing you, I don't think I want it. So you can keep your dowry."

The scream-shout that came from Bella next was deafening. Flora hadn't fully resumed her place in this realm and could hear it. Surely the entire Kingdom could too.

The parents did at least. The doors beyond the young couple flew open and the parents, along with the King's guard came in on a run.

"What is the meaning of this?" the King demanded as they all came to a stop.

Bella was pointing at the Prince, shrieking at the new arrivals. "He said we are not promised. He said he can take it back, that we won't be married. He said I'm ugly. He said he wouldn't have me as his wife. He said...He's...He's horrible." She wailed, running to her mother's arms.

"What is the meaning of THAT?!" Bella's father demanded, turning on the King.

The King and Queen exchanged glances before he spoke. "It means, that our son is not satisfied with our choice. He is old enough to make the decision. It seems that he has, though I have my doubts about the actual comments that were made. Perhaps it is time that you go." He offered.

"We'll be keeping the dowry!" Bella's mother shouted as they turned to go.

"We don't need your dowry. Save it for whomever

becomes her husband." Constantina answered softly, showing them to the door.

Flora fell on the floor in a fit of laughter as soon as she landed firmly in the main living space she shared with Fern. Sadly, Fern was not home to see it the show.

"That's why you need a Fairy Godmother." She announced to the vacant space. "To keep you from throwing your future away."

Sitting up, she realized that there was a decent chance she'd somehow be blamed for this too, even as she wasn't sure how. They had dismissed her. If they'd been worried about the meeting, they would have summoned her, right?

Chapter 6

Ariella's sixteenth birthday was celebrated with…nothing. No wishes, no treats, no presents. At least, not from anyone other than her father. In the late hours, after her step-mother and step-sisters had retired, he presented her with a small, simple, brown paper package.

"I know it isn't much, but these were your mothers. I've saved them aside for you." He said softly, kissing her fingertips as he placed the package in her hands across the table.

"Does she know?" Ariella asked before she could stop herself.

"She? She who? Your mother? No."

"I'm sorry. I shouldn't have asked. Thank you, for whatever they are." She offered graciously before she had even opened them.

Her father sighed, understanding dawning. "You mean your step-mother. No, she doesn't know either."

Carefully unwrapping the paper, Ariella gasped softly as two small, jeweled hair combs were revealed. "Papa, they're beautiful."

His replying smile was tinged with relief. "She would have wanted you to have them."

"My step-mother?" Ariella queried.

"No. Your mother."

"Thank you both. They are perfect."

The truth hung between them. Eventually, he broke the silence and spoke it. "You should hide them away. I don't have anything of the like to give your sisters, or your step-mother, and they should not get these. They might be jealous, and for that I'm sorry, but these should be yours."

"I understand." Ariella said quietly, just above a whisper, knowing she would need to find a worthy hiding place, though there were few.

It would become one of the last lingering conversations between her and her father. True to Fern's prediction, before the winter ended and the calendar turned, he took ill and didn't recover. Things really changed then.

Before the soil over his grave could settle, Ariella became more servant than anything else in the house. Her room, though always sparse, became more-so as she was relocated to a small alcove off the attic space. There was only room for a bed and a single dressing table.

Not that she had anything that resembled help before, she had none now. Every duty to be done, fell squarely, and solely, on her shoulders. Rising well before daybreak, and often working until long after the midnight chimes, her days were filled with work.

While her sisters were given private lessons, Ariella tried to teach herself from their discarded pages, the ones waiting to become fuel for the hearth. Though she did an admirable job, and efficiently completed every task she was given, it was never enough. Often, though she could never say so, her sisters would undo her efforts, just to add to the tally.

She often wept herself to sleep after gazing on her hair combs. They were the sole reminder of the affection of her parents. She tucked them away each time, deep into the stuffing of her thin mattress, the only place she could think to hide them. One day, she would wear them, far away from here. Until then, she heeded her father's words from over a year before, and kept them to herself.

Flora was busy ducking as Fern was busy throwing things.

"It's not fair." She shouted as she lobbed another piece of miscellaneous clay.

"That was mine." Flora interjected.

"Get over it. We can easily summon another anytime. This isn't about you." Fern snapped back, grabbing another random bit of anything breakable. "They are going to kill her like they did her father, and she's alone, Flora. Alone."

"No. She's not you tittering twit. She has you."

"Fat lot of good it does her. I cannot aid with the overload of chores they've put upon her. I cannot undo their daily cruelty." Fern growled out. "She has me….hmmmph."

"What would you do?" Flora glared impatiently, adding before Fern could reply. "Honestly, what would you do? You know as well as I that if she were able to finish and have more time, they would only find more for her to do. All you would succeed in accomplishing is giving them an opening to do worse. This, while horrid, must bear out."

Fern paused before her forward throwing motion went through, bringing the piece to rest in her free hand. "I hate it when you're right."

"Yes, I know."

"Did you know they've taken to dressing her in rags? She isn't even allowed decent clothing. The poor girl is going to die from exposure."

"Which is where you come in. You'll have to keep that from happening. She just needs to survive."

Fern rolled her eyes, landing in a hard stare at Flora. "You say that like it's so simple."

"It is Fern. The hard part is not getting caught."

His Royal Highness,

Prince Christopher Ladislaus Leopold,

Is giving a ball.

By order of the King and Queen...

The presence of every available maiden in

the Kingdom is hereby requested.

Harvest Eve

Eight O'clock.

Chapter 8

Ariella beamed. The official who had come announced the invitation loudly, before leaving a copy for the household.

"Every available maiden…that means me." She chirped happily.

"Mother, she can't possibly." One of the step-sisters began wailing loudly.

The other joined in quickly. "A royal ball is no place for a girl like you." She sneered at Ariella.

"Cinder…Ariella is correct," her step-mother said loudly over the girls, "it says 'Every' available maiden." She turned to Ariella. "You will be responsible for if you are available that evening though. Your chores must be completed."

"Oh, I will." Ariella replied gleefully, missing the sideways glance and brief nods between her step-mother and sisters.

It would be of no matter. Ariella would quickly come to realize that there was little chance that she would get to go. The other three women had her busier than ever.

Her normal duties usually ran her to the quick. The new ones, helping her sisters prepare, were often more than she could manage. Most days, she fell fast asleep at the kitchen table, too tired to climb the stairs to her tiny room.

Before long, she was leaner than ever, and looked every bit as worn as she was. She quickly learned that she would have to become a seamstress too. New bolts of beautiful fabric were delivered for her sister's dresses. No patterns, just fabric, although none for her. Ariella was tasked with transforming it into lavish gowns, and was warned by her step-mother, "Do not sabotage these dresses, or I will surely know." As though Ariella would have considered such an act.

She worked until her fingers bled from being poked repeatedly with pins and sewing needles. She was careful not to bleed on the fabric, but it was a difficult task. She did the best that she could manage, and was quite impressed with herself by the time she was done months later. Though the dresses were lovely, the sisters complained, traded, and whined some more before finally agreeing to wear them.

They had been starving themselves for days to fit into them, even though they had been made to size. Ariella hardly needed to worry over her weight, she couldn't keep any on if she tried. She only hoped that it would be over soon and she could return to her normal list of chores.

The night before the ball, while serving dinner to her step-mother and sisters, her step-mother paused to address her. "Have you decided what you will wear, Cinderella?"

Ariella winced at the name, knowing it was used to bait her. "Yes. I have a gown that was my mother's. I hope it will be good enough." She answered, trying not to sound too excited.

"Fetch it here."

Cautiously, Ariella retreated to her room to claim the dress, returning with it in her arms. "Will this do?" she asked.

Her sisters both wrinkled their noses at his. Her step-mother too gave the dress a disapproving glance. It was simple, but pretty. "It will have to unless you have another choice." She finally said.

Before she could think to stop herself, Ariella said, "I thought I could dress it up with my mother's combs."

"Combs? What combs?" her step-mother asked staring her down.

"My hair combs." She hedged, realizing her slip too late.

"Let's see these combs of yours."

Ariella felt sick. She shouldn't have said anything, but the cat was out of the bag now. She retreated to her room to get the hair combs. Reaching deep into her mattress, she felt from top to bottom but could not find them. She panicked, tossing the covers back and dumping the slight fill all about the room. They were gone.

When she returned to the table, her step-mother and sisters were snickering. It should have been the tip-off, but it wasn't. She stood, forcing herself not to weep openly. "They're gone. I don't know where they went. I always put them away, but they are missing."

"Where were they?" her step-mother asked in an odd tone.

Ariella's head dropped. "I kept them in my mattress."

"Why would you put them there?"

"To keep them safe."

"Safe from what?"

"Being taken."

"I guess it wasn't a very safe place then."

"But who would have taken them? No one goes to my room but me." Ariella sniffled, trying to keep from crying openly.

Her step-mother had obviously tired of her game by the look on her face before she spoke. "I would. I found them, and sold them to buy the fabric for your sister's dresses. Thank you so much for that. We really couldn't have afforded it any other way."

Ariella's mouth dropped with each word. They were gone? "My combs? Those were not yours to sell." She stammered out.

"Everything in this house is mine to sell should I see the need." Her step-mother admonished. "You should not have hidden them from me."

"They were my mother's. Get them back." She tried to demand.

"Ah. Ah. Ah. That will not do. Perhaps it is not your dress, but your attitude that does not belong at a royal ball. I think you can stay home." She leveled.

Ariella was devastated all over again. Racing from the room, she fled the house and went to be alone in the empty stables. The horses too had been sold since her father past. The structure was the only thing left.

"Here's your chance." Flora announced proudly to Fern when news of the ball reached them. "You can help your girl to win the prince."

"That is not our power. You know that. We can only help them to become the best of themselves. It must already be within her to win the prince Flora." Fern retorted.

"Yes, but she is fair, and gentle, and kind…is she not?"

"She is. Though I daresay they have tried to take that from her too."

"Then you really don't need to do much. Just arrange for the meeting to happen." Flora reasoned.

"That may be a tall order."

"What do you mean?"

"The step-mother. She is evil. She manages to cut the girl down without thought. The one thing the girl had, she has just learned was taken from her too. I don't know if I can mend that kind of emotional damage." Fern lamented.

"You can. If any of us can, it's you." Flora bolstered.

"I can try." Fern said doubtfully. "I can try."

Chapter 9

Word of the ball reached the Beaufort home. Bella determined immediately that she would be there. She would show Prince Christopher just what he was missing out on, and remind him that he was promised to her.

Weeks on end were spent with everyone in the household fretting about. Bella changed her mind on her dress no fewer than a dozen times, though probably more. The finest everything was acquired and finally worked into a dazzling dress, travelling cloak, and matching golden slippers, trimmed with fur.

A new carriage was purchased as well. The old one, though gilt and beautiful, was not acceptable to Bella, and her parents were doubling over trying to please her as much as the servants. The horses too were groomed and re-groomed in anticipation. Only when Bella approved, were they allowed to rest in anticipation of harvest night.

It still was not enough. Bella wanted more. She was nearly, but not yet eighteen, and thus, she knew, she still had a Fairy Godmother. She may have dismissed her, but she had to be nearby. "Floooorrraaahhhhh." She bellowed.

Flora's head hung low before she crossed over. She had been waiting for this. Arriving before Bella, there was no clue that she did not wish to be present. "You called?"

"I want you to make me beautiful." Bella demanded.

"I cannot." Flora replied factually.

"You can. You just don't want to."

"No. I cannot. I can only help you to become what you already are. Are you beautiful?"

"Of course I'm beautiful." Bella snipped. "That's not what I mean."

"That's what you said."

"I mean, make me irresistible."

"I cannot do that either."

"You're impossible Flora."

Flora didn't respond.

"Fine!" Bella finally recanted. "Tell me how to become irresistible."

"I cannot say. I don't believe I know that."

"You do. Make the Prince fall in love with me."

"I most certainly cannot do that."

Bella scream-squealed. "What *CAN* you do?"

"I've already answered that. I can help you to become what you already are."

"What's that?"

"You tell me."

"I'm rich."

"Then you don't need me for that."

"I'm beautiful."

"Again, don't need me for that."

"Then how do you make me become what I already am?" Bella whined.

Flora shrugged. "That's an excellent question. Once upon a time, I would have said by guiding you to behaviors and graces, and such…but now, as I've not been part of those formative years, you have already become what you will be."

"Flora, you're impossible."

"No. I was dismissed. I suppose now the only thing left is to see you safely to the ball, and make sure you stay out of trouble."

"I'm sure I don't need you for that."

"Then perhaps you don't need me after all."

"Ohhhhhh. You'd like that wouldn't you. You'd get to brag to all your Fairy Godmother friends about how I released you and then what…failed?" Bella goaded.

"I don't think that's how it works. Give it a try."

"Oh no you don't. You're going to go to the ball with me." Bella announced triumphantly, not realizing she'd been manipulated. "You'll see. I'll win the Prince and the Kingdom, and it will be because of me. Not you. Me."

"As you wish."

She shouldn't, but Flora couldn't help herself. She rolled back and forth across the rug, rocking with hard laughter. Fern waiting patiently for the break to find out what was so funny.

"Oh Fern, you should have seen her face. Her pinched up, frustrated, 'I know everything,' face. She wanted to be made beautiful, and irresistible. She wanted me…ME, to make the Prince fall in love with her. She knows nothing." She finally got out between gasps for air between more laughter.

"What did you do?"

"I got her to take me to the ball."

"To what end?"

Flora stopped laughing. She stared her sister down for a few moments, thinking Fern would catch on. She didn't. "To bear witness to the madness. She has learned nothing, Fern. NOTHING. She thinks she's going to traipse into a ball she wasn't invited to and walk out with the Prince on her arm. I want to watch. It's going to be epic. Sad, but epic."

"That's not nice Flora."

"No. It's not. But, it is the eventual outcome of the events that have played out. Why should I be denied the finale?"

Fern tapped her chin. "I suppose there really aren't any rules against it."

"Nope. Not a single one." Flora chirped. "I checked. As long as I don't interfere in the course of the events between them, I'm not out of line."

"But you're not going to help either?"

"I cannot intervene between two people. It is, as it has always been. I can coach her, encourage her, even dress her up...but at the end, it has to be HER that wins him...no magic."

Fern's eyes lit up. Flora noticed, sitting up quickly before lying back when her head started to spin. "What are you thinking?"

"Just thinking." Fern replied coyly.

"You're up to something."

"Maybe." Fern grinned back. "But don't say it like that. You make it sound like you're not."

"Oh. I definitely am. I am up to seeing this girl, once again, blow it."

"Flora!" Fern admonished.

"Tell me you wouldn't. If you had one of those brat step-sisters who were so busy making someone else miserable...tell me you wouldn't sit back and let the events play out. Go on...tell me that." Flora asserted, finally able to sit up fully.

Fern hedged. "I might. But…I don't know that I would take such pleasure from knowing it was coming.

"That's you."

"Yes. But not you."

"Right." Flora beamed. "So tell me what you have planned.

Chapter 10

Ariella was surely going to be severely punished for not going in the day of the ball to help her sisters. She couldn't bear it. It was all she could do to sit still and not run far away from the only home she had ever known. Long past dim, the sounds of the carriage and horses no longer heard beyond the stalls in the drive, she raised herself up and moved to leave the stables. The crack of a branch beyond the gate stopped her short.

"Who's there?" She called out softly, hoping for no reply.

"Fern."

Peeking her head out, Ariella squinted to focus on the tiny woman standing just beyond the stables. "Fern who?"

"Oh, tut-tut now. Come out and we'll meet again."

"Again? I'm sure I've never met anyone named Fern." Ariella replied pensively.

"You were a baby. I suppose you wouldn't count that since you probably can't recall it."

Ariella eyed her suspiciously. "A baby? You were here?"

"I was. I am your Fairy Godmother."

"Fairy Godmother?! Where have you been all my life? I've been through hell. Have you been watching? I really could have used you a bunch of times."

Fern blushed in embarrassment. "Yes, I've been watching. I wish that helping was part of the deal that way. It isn't. My job is to keep you out of trouble until you're of age, and to guide you to become the best version of you that you can be." She shrugged. "You didn't need me for that. You are kind, to a fault I might add. Generous, though you have little to give. And selfless, which is something that I cannot teach you if you don't have it within you. To be blunt…it was you who didn't need me. I've waited all your life for you to have a need I could fill."

Ariella had come out and sat on a stone near Fern as she spoke. "And what would that be?"

"To get you to the ball." Fern replied brightly.

"I can't go to the ball." Ariella bemoaned slouching.

"Why ever not?"

"The carriage has left. I didn't come out. Besides, my step-mother has already said 'no.'"

"Welllll…we just won't tell her then." Fern whispered conspiratorially.

"I'm sure she would recognize me Fern. I'm not that hard to spot. I stick out like a sore thumb."

"We can fix that too. But, we need to hurry or you'll arrive in time to leave again."

Ariella sighed wistfully. "I do want to see the castle."

"Then let's get moving girl! Time is wasting. Go get your dress on." Fern directed.

As Ariella ran inside, Fern gave her wand a soft flick in the general direction of the largest pumpkin in the patch. As she watched, the vines wound in upon themselves, forming into large ornate wheels and a base, lifting the pumpkin up off the ground. Ariella stopped in her tracks as she came back outside, awestruck to watch a golden carriage being formed before her eyes.

She blinked rapidly. Multiple tears had already tracked her face. The sight of the carriage halted them. She watched Fern busily turning field mice into attendants before she reached her side too.

"This is beautiful, but I can't go." She cried.

"Of course you can." Fern countered before looking. "Why aren't you in your dress?"

Ariella's sobs returned full force as she held up the destroyed dress. The fabric was burned and falling apart. Her step-mother, or one of her sisters, had hung it before the hearth and let it catch. "It's ruined." Ariella cried. "It was simple before, but now it's not usable at all. It's impossible."

"Pish-posh. Put it on. I can't make something out of nothing…only something out of something else. Impossible things happen every day if you know where to look." Fern retorted. "I'll turn my head. Do it here, we don't have time to waste."

Ariella was doubtful, but did as instructed.

When Fern turned back, her face said it all. The dress was irreparable. "Consider it their gift to you." She announced before giving her wand a wiggle.

Ariella blanched to see the wand waved at her. She was suddenly nervous, and doubtful about this course of action. "Are you sur..." She began, not quite finishing her question.

Like being tugged in a wind tunnel, Ariella felt herself lifted, as the fabric of her dress shifted against her skin. When she set down to right again, she was dumbstruck. In place of the tattered rags of what was left of her mother's dress, was an incredible emerald gown like she had never seen. The worn hide of her slippers too had changed. Lifting the dress, she spied two tiny glass ones in their place.

"I…I…I don't know what to say." She stammered out.

"Say you like it." Fern replied, grinning.

"Like it? No, Fern, no. I love it." Ariella beamed. "Are you sure they won't know it's me?"

"I'm positive. One, because you aren't supposed to be

there. Two, because they know there is nothing like this dress in the home they share with you. And three, because they have never seen you. Not really anyway. We'll clean you up good and I bet they'll never guess."

Ariella thrummed with excitement watching the finishing touches as they came together.

"Now," Fern drew her attention. "remember this is temporary. You have until the last chime of midnight before the magic is broken and everything goes back the way it was…dress, pumpkin…everything. Understand?"

"Oh yes. Yes, I do." Ariella said nodding.

"One last thing." Fern bit back a rogue tear. "My gift to you." She held out a small box.

"I couldn't possibly. You've given me too much already. Thank you for all of it." Ariella declined the gift.

"I insist." Fern retorted, opening the box to reveal Ariella's mother's hair combs.

"What have you done?" Ariella gasped.

"I've set right a wrong." Fern answered. "They are not magic, but you might want to do a better job of hiding them this time."

Fern bounced upon the roof of the carriage all the way to the ball. Upon arrival, she climbed down and went to find Flora who was already there. The night was sure to be filled with plenty to see, not the least of which was Flora's girl making a mess of things.

Fern hoped though that the real show would be Ariella getting everything that she deserved but had been denied. It was time.

Chapter 11

Bella was in a red rage. She had arrived in high fashion, only to go un-noticed by anyone but the doorman. She'd traipsed past Prince Christopher no less than a half-dozen times, but he hadn't so much as acknowledged she was there. She placated herself with the notion that he didn't realize it was her…which only served to infuriate her further a moment later because he seemingly wasn't curious to find out who she was.

This was all going dreadfully wrong, again. And, it wasn't like she could summon Flora. Everyone in the ball would surely hear her, even over the music and chatter. She was failing, again.

She had finally plucked up the nerve to dim her rage and approach the Prince when a young woman entered, drawing everyone's attention. Especially his. Dressed in a stunning emerald green gown that matched her eyes, she was breathtaking, but didn't seem to notice it as she stared openly at the opulence of the castle.

The woman was petite and within a moment, Bella had to strain on tip-toe to catch a glimpse of her. Everyone else was doing the same as a small crowd had encircled her. Bella's rage was rekindled from one breath to the next at the resumed lack of attention. What was she doing wrong?

She tried everything. She mimicked the actions and seeming wonder of the new woman, nothing. She tried to appear disinterested in the crowd, but only found herself alone as no one had noticed her ploy. She couldn't understand why she was not getting any attention, and was so lost in her own thoughts that she tripped over a pair of girls who were also openly gawking at the new woman.

"Watch where you're going." One clipped out, pulling her dress from beneath Bella's feet.

"I'm sorry. I didn't see you there."

"Obviously." The second one sneered.

"I beg your pardo..."

"Begging is for servants." The second one interrupted before Bella finished.

"Or Cinderella." The first remarked snidely.

"Who?" Bella enquired, not thinking to walk away.

"That's for us to know." One said,

The other added, "And you to wonder."

They linked arms and sashayed off, leaving Bella standing alone.

"Great." She commented to no one. "I can't even have company with the mean girls. This was a mistake."

Irritated, she made her way around the perimeter to the entrance, slipping out, but not before noticing Prince Christopher dancing with the woman in emerald. They were handsome together. Wishing for her turn was going to be a lost cause and she knew it.

Ducking out the front door, she stopped short. At the foot of the stairs was the most elaborate, beautiful carriage she had ever seen. Once again, her temper flared. It was unacceptable that there should be a better one that wasn't hers. "Impossible." She snipped loudly into the night. "It's impossible."

Without stopping to think of right and wrong, she descended the stairs and slipped into the golden buggy, smarting off to the coachmen as she closed the door.

"Drive." She directed. It wouldn't hurt for her to just take it for a little ride. The girl already got the Prince, that much she was sure of. She wouldn't mind or miss her carriage for a bit. She was going to be busy dancing for the night anyway, Bella was certain.

Flora watched Bella leave the ball, and then again as she slid into the magic carriage her sister had created. Hysterical laughter bloomed, forcing her to leave the premises for a bit to shake it loose. Oh what a surprise Bella would be in for, and soon.

Chapter 12

Ariella was swept away the moment she exited the carriage. The castle was beyond her wildest dreams as she looked up to see it turned out in favors and lights that twinkled. She had seen it before, but only from the distance. She'd never had reason to be so close.

She ducked in behind the attendant at the front door, certain that her ruse would be blown if she had to be announced to the room. It was temporarily successful. Nearly from the moment she crossed into the large gathering, she felt as though every head in the room had turned to see her. This would be more difficult than she'd imagined. She would need to locate her step-mother and sisters quickly to know where they were to avoid them.

Looking around the massive crowd, she had difficulty spotting them. She was soon surrounded by a group of people all introducing themselves and commenting on her dress. The attention was unsettling.

She spent long moments apologizing for missing comments as she tried to deftly look beyond the crowd. Eventually she spotted them, on the far side of the room. She only needed to keep tabs on them now and remain opposite.

A young man offered her his arm. Without thinking, she took it and was whirled onto the dance floor. He was quite good looking, and very adept. She felt like she was floating.

"I've never seen you before." He offered quietly.

"I've never been here before."

"That must be it." He laughed off. "Are you from the village?"

"Nearby, yes." Ariella hedged.

For what surely felt like hours, he led her in every dance, passing the time with quiet talk between them. Ariella was surprised that no one cut in for a turn. She decided it was better that way. Less chances to slip up.

She enjoyed herself immensely. Far too soon, it was over. The large clock began chiming. She almost forgot to notice the time until the hour was halfway marked.

"Oh. I'm afraid I must go." She stammered, pulling away.

He reached for her hand as it slipped away, but missed. "But the ball isn't over." He called as she dashed off.

Ariella didn't look back. The eighth chime was sounding as she made it to the entrance doorway. She was going to be cutting it close.

"Tell me your name." She heard him call as she descended the stairs.

At what point she lost her shoe, she couldn't say. There was not a second to think about, or look for it. She panicked as she reached the bottom. Her carriage was gone.

A small woman who reminded her of Fern, but wasn't, was waving franticly. "Take this one. You must go…now." She yelled.

Ariella didn't hesitate, slipping into the stunning carriage, pulling the door closed as it lurched forward and away.

"That was close." She uttered to herself as she felt the wisps of magic disintegrating around her. By the time she reached home, all that was left of the magic was a single glass slipper. She removed it, tucking it into her pocket before exiting the carriage.

"What do I do with you?" She wondered aloud.

"Go home." She announced to the horses, as though they could follow directions. They didn't.

She debated hiding the carriage and horses in the stables, even as she knew they would be found. They couldn't stay in the lane, that much was certain. She ducked inside, intending to change, but racing out again when she heard hooves on the gravel, thinking her step-mother and sisters had returned before she could get rid of the carriage.

She was mistaken. It wasn't them. It was a group of the King's regiment. "Oh no." She gasped. They'll think I've stolen it.

When the gathering came to a halt in the middle of the drive, they parted. At the center was the young man who had been dancing with her. Ariella began to shake.

"Did you see the young woman who rode in this carriage?" He asked before dismounting.

"I...."

"Did you hear him?" One of the attendants added. "Answer the Prince."

"The Prince?!" Ariella stammered, curtseying low.

When she rose, he was standing before her. "Would a mirror help?" He asked, sounding amused.

"Would a what?"

"It's you, isn't it?"

"I..."

Ariella couldn't see Fern standing behind and beyond her, nodding furiously in response to the question she herself couldn't answer. She flushed from head to foot.

"Bring me that slipper." The Prince commanded to the attendant who had rebuked her.

Ariella watched as he dismounted, carrying the small glass shoe carefully, but not carefully enough. He tripped on the loose gravel, and it fell, shattering into even smaller pieces.

The Prince sighed. "I guess we will never know."

"Oh yes we will." Fern interjected, rushing up and reaching into Ariella's pocket to withdraw the other one. "Put it on." She urged Ariella.

Ariella swallowed a hard lump. "But…"

"Please, will you put it on?" The Prince asked.

"It's only a shoe." Ariella whispered.

"I need to see it. Please." He pleaded.

"But why?"

"Because, if it is you, you are the one for me. I was just another face in the crowd, not a crown to be claimed to you tonight. You were yourself, and no one does that with me."

"But we've only just met. I don't know you."

"Would you like to?"

"Well…yes."

"Then put on the shoe. My name is Christopher."

Ariella slipped her foot into the tiny slipper. As soon as the heel clicked on, the lingering magic swirled about them both, revealing her, once again, in her emerald dress, just as lovely as she had been earlier.

"It's you!" He said excitedly.

"It's me." She answered softly.

She was swept up in a spin before he landed a quick kiss on her lips that seared her to her toes. They broke apart, her blushing furiously, he laughing.

"Say you'll be mine."

"I don't…"

"She will." Fern interjected, finishing with a laugh. "Good grief, do I have to do all the hard parts?"

"But what about…" Ariella hesitated.

"I should ask…" The Prince began.

"He's dead." Ariella answered, assuming he was going to say 'your father.'"

"Oh. Well, that too…but I was going to say I should ask your name."

Ariella's jaw dropped and she turned away, embarrassed.

"Her name's Cinderella." One of her step-sisters chimed in before Ariella could turn back.

"It is not!" Ariella demanded.

"Then what is it?" The Prince asked again.

"My father named me Ariella."

"Then Ariella, will you be mine?"

"Yes she will." Fern stated emphatically when Ariella couldn't find words.

She was too busy watching the face of her step-mother and sisters. They were obviously quite put out with her. She hadn't heard them arrive.

"I…I…Yes." She finally managed, enjoying the shock that played across her step-mother's face as a fire lit her eyes.

"You. Will. Not." Her step-mother demanded. "You are my ward, and I forbid it." She turned to the Prince. "You may choose one of my daughters though." She added sweetly.

The Prince turned to reply, but Ariella finally found her tongue. "It's after midnight. I'm eighteen. And I say…YES."

Prince Christopher beamed. "That works for me. We can take your things, or come back for them. I'd like to return to the ball and present you…as my Princess-to-be."

"There's nothing left here for me." Ariella admitted, trying not to sound pathetic.

The Prince looked at her step-mother. "I would like to be surprised by that, but I'm not. Perhaps we should take the carriage as your dowry."

"It's not mine."

"Oh, then we should return it to its owner. Will you join me?" He asked, offering his arm.

"I would like that very much, but I need to thank someone first."

Fern was standing to her side as she turned. "Pish-posh. Go. I'll be around. Not that you need me now…just because I want to see you get what you deserve."

With that, Prince Christopher helped her into the carriage as his horse was tethered to the lead, and they were off. Ariella didn't look back.

Fern and Flora slapped each other's hands in the air, jumping with excitement before slipping to their personal space.

"You did it!" Flora exclaimed.

"Nope. Not me. Ariella did it." Fern replied. "Though I'm not sure that was what she planned to do."

"Which is why it worked." Flora yelped. "Good things DO happen."

"Impossible things even." Fern grinned.

"Yes. That too."

"But I should thank you."

"Me?"

"You think I don't know who guided Ariella to the other carriage?"

"What choice was there? I know your magic, she didn't have time. Besides, I know where the carriage you made was, and there was no way she was going to get to it."

"You know where it is?"

"I do."

"How's that?"

"Because I watched Bella take it. She had no idea of course that it was magic and wouldn't last, or she might not have. But, it set things up nicely for Ariella to be unable to quite slip away."

"She took it?"

"She did."

"Where is it now?"

"Uhhhhmmmmmm."

Chapter 13

Bella shrieked as the carriage creaked and shuddered. "Oh God! I'm going to die…I'm going to die…I'm going to die." She yelped out as the ball portion came off the wheels and bounced along the cobbled road, finally resting upright with a splatting sound, and an odd fractured hole where the window used to be.

"What the hell is this?" She screamed into the darkness.

No one answered.

She reached for the door handle. It, like the window, was gone. What came back between her fingers was slime-y and stringy. If there had been light she might have looked closer. Then again, she might not have.

She made her way to the odd-shaped opening, and the only light. Looking out, she couldn't make out much. Only the outline of houses beyond a single, dim, lamp-light.

"Hello??? Hell…looooo-oh?" she screamed through the opening, hoping someone would hear her. She kept screaming for what felt like hours, though likely wasn't.

"Hello? Who called?" A voice finally called back, breaking the silence.

"Me! In here." Bella answered excitedly. "My carriage came apart and I cannot get out. I need help. Can you assist me?" Bella shouted through the narrow opening.

"I can hear you."

Bella jammed her fingers through the rough hole and wiggled them. "Here! Can you see my fingers?? I'm in here. I need help. I can't get out."

"Woah. How'd you get in there?"

"It's my carriage..."

"Really? It doesn't look like a carriage."

"Well it WAS a carriage. It did a lot of bouncing. I'm sure it's broken now. Can you get me out?"

"Gosh. I really don't know."

"Could you try?"

"Maybe. My name's Peter."

"Bella."

"Hey Bella...you know what? This looks like a pumpkin."

"Fabulous."

"I ***LIKE*** pumpkin."

"FLORRRRRRRAAAAAAAAHHHHHH!"

Fern heard the bellowed summons, just as Flora winced. "Aren't you going to answer her?"

"Nope."

"Nope?" Fern queried.

Flora grinned broadly. "Perk of position...or former position."

"Oh?"

"Oh yes. As Ariella is eighteen, so is Bella. I'm not responsible for her anymore."

Fern's eyes went wide. "And you're okay with that?"

"More than okay. Call it consequences."

Fern raised a quizzical eyebrow. "How so?"

Flora snickered openly, replying in rhyme-scheme.

"Peter, Peter, pumpkin eater, took a wife but couldn't free her, left her in a pumpkin shell, and there he hid her, very well."

Watch for more
Flip-Flopped Fairy Tales

<u>**Three Wishes**</u>

(from Aladdin & the Lamp)

<u>**'Untitled'**</u>

(from The 12 Dancing Princesses)

Other titles by Savannah Verte

Viva Zapata & the Magic 8-Ball

The Custos Series:

Book of Time

Book of Change

Book of Mysteries
(September 12, 2017)

C.A.S.E. Revelations

Tales in 13 Chapters:

Immortal Deflagration

Immortal Alchemy

Rogue
(Cimmerian Shade box set September 12, 2017)

Gravedigger
(September 30, 2017)

Veil Break
(Haunting Savannah box set October 10, 2017)

The Vengelys Series Complete Set
(2017-2018 release pending w/Aedan Byrnes)

About The Author

A lifelong lover of words and reading, Savanah Verte hasn't quite figured out what she wants to write when she grows up. Born and raised in the upper Midwest, Savannah's gypsy spirit and never quit attitude keep her busy and seldom idle. For so many reasons, Savannah considers herself a 'Contemporary Vagabond' when it comes to writing and hopes that others find her diverse offerings as enjoyable to read as they are to write.

As the primary owner and driving force behind Eclectic Bard Books, she considers herself immensely fortunate to see writing from varied perspectives as she endeavors to publish the authors rostered there. Working with other writers, Savannah gets to expand her horizons every day as someone brings a new idea to the table and the brainstorming begins. There is something addictive about the creative process for her and helping other authors embrace their dreams make hers a reality daily.

Follow Savannah:

www.savannahverte.com

www.facebook.com/authorsavannahverte

www.eclecticbardbooks.com/savannahverte

EB
www.eclecticbardbooks.com

Made in the USA
Columbia, SC
01 March 2018